Infinite Waters: 9+1 Speculative Fiction Short Stories

INFINITE WATERS

9+1 Speculative Fiction Short Stories

NICHOLAS C. ROSSIS

Infinite Waters: 9+1 Speculative Fiction Short Stories

Nicholas C. Rossis

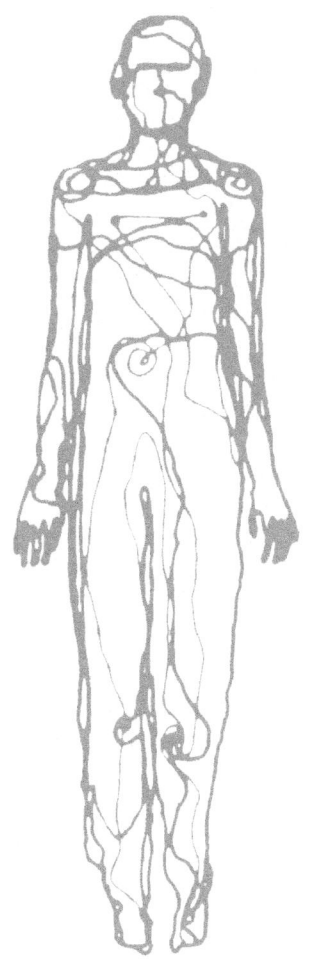

ISBN: 978-1514771396

Copyright © 2015 Nicholas C. Rossis. All rights reserved.

Illustrations by Dimitris Fousekis. Copyright © 2014 Dimitris Fousekis. All rights reserved.

Cover by Alexios Saskalidis, 187designz.deviantart.com. All rights reserved.

Editor: Lorelei Logsdon

Infinite Waters: 9+1 Speculative Fiction Short Stories

Nicholas C. Rossis

We create our own narratives.

Then we live by them.

Infinite Waters: 9+1 Speculative Fiction Short Stories

Contents

CONTENTS 9
INFINITE WATERS 11
THE THINGS WE DO FOR LUST 15
INFINITE WATERS 23
JAMES' LIFE 25
INFINITE WATERS 27
TWO'S A CROWD 29
INFINITE WATERS 45
WHAT'S IN A NAME? 47
INFINITE WATERS 55
THE LUCKY BASTARD 57
INFINITE WATERS 63
A TWIST OF THE TAIL 65
INFINITE WATERS 73
IS THERE A DOCTOR IN THE HOUSE? 75
INFINITE WATERS 81
SEX AND DINNER 83
INFINITE WATERS 85
WOULD YOU LIKE FLIES WITH THAT? 87
INFINITE WATERS 95
FURTHER STORIES 99
The Power of Six: 6+1 Science Fiction Short Stories 101

THE HAND OF GOD 103
A NOTE FROM THE AUTHOR 113
ABOUT THE AUTHOR 117
ACKNOWLEDGMENTS 119
FURTHER NOTES 121

Infinite Waters: 9+1 Speculative Fiction Short Stories

Infinite Waters

"That will be ten dollars."

The woman clutched her leather purse for a second, then snapped it open and fished out a battered wallet that had seen better days. She passed me a crumpled bill, an apologetic look on her face. I almost told her to keep it, then remembered that I, too, had to pay bills.

I shoved the money into my pocket with my left hand, my right one already hovering over the divination tools. Which one would be required today? The answer depended partly on the question, partly on inspiration.

"What do you want to know?"

In the dim light of the tent, I saw her fidget with her purse. *Probably just another love-stricken woman*, I told myself. *Pity. She was cute. She deserved better than an unfaithful boyfriend or a brutish husband.*

I stared at my hands for a moment, then stole an inquisitive look at her. Like her wallet, she, too, had seen better days. The fine worry lines on her face betrayed a life of hardship. I listened to the howling wind outside, flapping the tent's awning, as I studied a broken plastic pin that held together her hair. The pin hung on to the thick golden and silver strands, like a drunk holding on to his last bottle, but I could see it was a losing battle.

I waited patiently, taking in the sweet smell of burning incense from the stick to my left. Her mouth opened, then closed again. I discreetly pushed the smoking stick farther away, so as not to derail her train of thought.

"I want to be..." she started, then stopped. "No." She jutted her jaw in defiance. "I am an author." Her self-confidence waned just as suddenly as it had appeared. "Or would like to be. Someday. Maybe."

An author. Not a love thing, then. At least, not in the sense I had thought. "Have you written anything?"

Her cheeks flushed. "I..." she stuttered. "I have. A book. I mean, of course it's a book, what else would it be? If I'm a writer. I am writing it. The book. Not right now, of course. I'm talking to you, not—"

I raised my hand to stop her, her train of thought obviously already derailed and plunging into a cliff, complete with screaming passengers and bawling train engineers. I hoped she wrote better than she spoke. "And you want to know if it will be a success?"

"I want inspiration. And that, of course. Success."

My lips parted into a smile. "I see." I reached under the table for a seldom-used item. My fingers touched soft fabric. I pulled out a round object on the table, draped in velvet, and placed it on the table. With a flourish, I removed the cover.

She put a hand over her mouth to hide her mirth. "A crystal ball?" She cocked her head and gave me a mischievous grin. "Isn't that a bit of a cliché?"

"Sure is." I pulled a soft cloth and wiped off a smudge from its surface. "Clichés exist for a reason."

"But—"

"Why don't you stare inside and tell me what you see?" I interrupted her.

Curiosity and disbelief fought in her eyes. Curiosity won. It always did.

Her expression changed from disbelief to wonder as she leaned forward and stared into the globe. A soft glow came from deep within. Shapes swirled and danced inside, luring her deeper and deeper into the infinite waters of a myriad universes...

Infinite Waters: 9+1 Speculative Fiction Short Stories

The Things We Do for Lust

"Alcmene?"

The spool slipped through my fingers and rolled onto the floor. I skipped over the thread and hurried down the stairs to rush into his arms. "You're home," I cried out as I barreled into the room. "I was so worried about you."

His tall frame stood against the open door, the sun showing off his muscular body. He glanced down at me, his soft brown eyes sparkling. He opened his arms and I jumped into his bear hug. I squeezed against him and kissed him, our lips melting together.

"I told you that I'd be safe, didn't I?" He pushed me gently away to unclasp his woolen cloak. Holding it on one arm, he held it high.

A slave hurried to accept the crimson garment. Underneath, Amphitryon still wore his leather armor.

I ran a trembling finger against it, checking for stains. Finding none, I let out a relieved sigh. A shudder ran along my back. "I was so worried."

Amphitryon sat on a bench and untied the leather straps on his leggings. No blood on them, either. He let out a sigh and rubbed the striped marks left on his calves. "Worried enough to show your husband some love?"

I raised a hand to my mouth to stifle my chuckle. *He's insatiable. Then again, that's why I love him so much.* Despite myself, excitement crept up my body. I had missed him more than I cared to admit. *Men and their stupid wars!* I leaned in and sniffed him. He smelled divine, but I played hard-to-get. I scrunched my nose. "Don't you need a bath first? You smell of the road."

He grabbed my hand and drew me into his lap. "What I need is my wife."

I yelped and then laughed. My cackle turned to soft moans as our tongues entwined in a fiery kiss. Shivers ran along my entire body. I slapped my palm against his chest and pushed him away for a moment, to catch my breath. My fingers caught on a chain around his neck. It held a strange stone. It seemed to shimmer and glow with an eerie light from within, misty shapes and colors shifting and twirling inside. "What's this?" I whispered. My voice betrayed my awe.

He waved his hand dismissively. "Spoils of war."

Before I could question him further, he rose to his feet, lifting me with him. I squealed and leaned against his chest, listening to the thudding of his heart as he hauled me into our room. His heel pushed against the door, slamming it shut behind us.

###

Hours later, a soft bump woke me up. "Amphitryon?"

"Sorry, love," his soft voice whispered. "Didn't mean to wake you."

I rubbed the sleep from my eyes. I had drifted asleep after our lovemaking. Heat crept up my cheeks as I remembered the details. *Best sex ever!*

He sat down on the bed, and I scooted towards the wall to give him more space. I yawned and stretched my arms. A cold gust of wind blew into the room, making my hairs stand on end. I draped my body with the sheet and peered outside the open window. There was little light coming from the night sky. Clouds had swallowed the moon, and the soft patter of rain echoed on the roof tiles. A lone lantern sent a warm orange light to chase shadows away from Amphitryon's handsome face. I traced his cheek with adoring fingers. "You're so handsome."

"Thank you," he said with a chuckle. "You're not so bad yourself."

I leaned towards him and planted a soft kiss on his mouth. He pushed his lips against mine with a surprising urgency. *Again?* My eyes widened, then I closed them and moaned as I let his tongue invade my mouth. *Well, if he's up for it, why not?* I threw him on the bed and straddled him, tearing off his gown with shaky hands.

He let out a deep, contented sigh. "That was amazing."

"Whatever possessed you, I like it," I murmured, a smile playing at my lips.

He stroked my naked arm, sending goosebumps on my skin. "Just my love for you."

"Aw, you always know what to say," I cooed. I pushed his arm upwards, to crawl underneath it. Snuggling like that always made me feel safe, secure. It was one of the things I loved most about him. *I couldn't have married a better man,* I thought, not for the first time. If I were a cat, I would start purring.

Instead, it was my stomach that growled, reminding me that we had spent the entire day in bed. "You must be starving. After all, I'm not the only one who skipped lunch."

He laughed. "True." He cocked his head to look down at me, a frown between his eyes. "Wait, how did you know I had no lunch?" He raised his hand to his mouth and blew into his palm. "My breath doesn't smell, does it?"

I chuckled. "No, silly! How could you have had lunch? Neither of us did."

He pushed his fingers through my hair in long strokes, releasing the scent of lavender. "You skipped lunch, too? Why?"

Huh? It was my turn to stare at him in confusion. "What do... Because we were here? Doing... you know..." I could feel my cheeks blush once again.

His hand stopped, caught in my hair. "Alcmene, I've only just arrived. I missed lunch to return as soon as I could, but it's been raining, and the roads were all muddy. The slaves told me you were sleeping, so I took a bath, then came upstairs."

The raindrops falling on the clay roof tiles suddenly filled the room like the beating of a drum. My mouth twitched. "But I saw your sandals. There was no mud on them. How…"

He touched my brow with the back his hand. "Are you all right? You seem flustered."

I pulled away, annoyed. *What's going on here?* "I… You…" My voice trailed off. I shook my head, as if to clear it from cobwebs inside. "You're saying you just got here?"

"Yes." His eyes were filled with worry, then his taut face relaxed. "You must have had a dream. The slaves said you haven't left the room all day. Were you sleeping?"

A dream? I nodded, forcing a smile on my lips. "Yes, that must be it. A dream."

"You did what?" the science officer shouted, barely hiding her irritation. She lifted up a hand. "Europa. Io. Semele. Callisto. Dione." With each name, she pointed at a finger. Realizing she had run out of them, she started from the thumb again. "Persephone. Nemesis. Thaleia. Danae. And now Alcmene?" She threw the captain an exasperated look. "Seriously, you need help. We didn't spend centuries developing time travel just so you can get your kicks."

"Aw, come on—what's the worst that can happen?" The captain swiveled himself on the couch in order to plant his feet up the armrest.

"Damn it, Captain. I'm a doctor, not a pimp."

The captain fixed her with sparkling blue eyes. "You're not a doctor, you're a science officer."

"With a doctorate," she barked.

The captain smirked. "Doesn't matter, really, does it? The timeline fixes itself. It always does."

She grabbed a tablet from the messy desk sitting at the corner of the captain's quarters. "We'll see about that." She stabbed the screen with an angry finger. It came to life, spewing data. She lifted her gaze to the ceiling. "Great. Now there's another one."

His eyes widened. He swiveled his feet back on the shining floor. "I have another kid?"

"Sure." She showed him the tablet. "A son. Alcides."

He snatched the tablet from her outstretched arm and read. His face lit up. "Alcides. Nice."

"No, not nice!" The officer pinched the bridge of her nose and squeezed. "You're sick. As soon as we're back, I have to report this. You know that, don't you?"

"No one cares," he said with a shrug. "As long as the timeline's intact, what difference does it make? Just leave out the details."

"Oh, believe me, no one wants to know any details after Danaes' golden shower—"

"Golden *rain*."

"Whatever." She paced the room in furious steps. "As for no one caring, what about your wife?"

"Let me worry about her." The captain threw the tablet across the room. It landed on the desk and slid on it until it bumped against a monitor.

She walked over and picked it up again. "Honestly, I don't see what she sees in you. I suppose you used that ridiculous moniker again?"

"Actually, I never introduced myself. She thought I was her husband."

"Her..." She spun around to face the captain. "You used a cloaking amulet on the poor woman? Glamour is for emergencies only!"

"This *was* an emergency," the captain said with a sigh. "You should have seen her. Largest—"

The officer raised a hand to stop him. "Don't want to know."

"*Eyes* I've ever seen. Anyway. All that matters is that I gave her something her husband never could."

She stared at the screen. "Is that right? Because it says right here that she's expecting twins. Apparently, hubby came home right after you." She pointed at the tablet. "See? Right here. 'Heteropaternal superfecundation'."

The captain arched an eyebrow. "I saw that. Thought it was a typo."

"A t..." The officer glared at the captain. "That's when a woman carries twins sired by different fathers. You both had sex with her on the same night. She's carrying two sons. One by you. One by her husband."

"Oh, right," the captain said with a shrug. "My bad."

Her eyes almost popped out of their sockets. "You're the most irresponsible, reckless, immature—"

The captain stifled a yawn. "You start sounding like my wife, and I'm exhausted. Alcmene really was something else."

She closed her eyes and counted to ten, drawing deep breaths. Then, she whirled around and stomped towards the door. It swished open. Before stepping through, she turned around once again. "What do you want to do with the boy? Any special gifts?"

"Oh, right." The captain rubbed his chin. "What did we do last time?"

"Prophecy. A simple enough gift to bestow, if you're a time-traveler."

"Hmm..." The captain stared blankly for a few moments, then snapped his fingers. "I know. Let's go for brawns this time. How strong can you make him?"

"With the latest advances in bionics? *Very* strong. But what about your wife?"

"Tell you what. Let's have them rename Alcides. We'll call him Heracles, after her. Maybe that will placate her."

"I'm sure it will make all the difference in the world," she said drily, as she stepped through the door and into the spotless, narrow corridor. "Father of the gods, my cockadoodle," she murmured under her breath.

Infinite Waters

The woman jerked backwards, a stunned look on her face. *"What was that?"*

I couldn't help but chuckle at her reaction. *"Inspiration."*

Our gazes locked, a newfound fire burning in her eyes. *"Can you show me more?"*

I purse my lips. Their edges twitch upwards, then I nod.

Infinite Waters: 9+1 Speculative Fiction Short Stories

Nicholas C. Rossis

James' Life

James was not a happy man. He had lost much in his life, and then some. Lost his parents as a child, then ran into troubles with the law. His personal life was even worse; one bad, ephemeral relationship after another. Trouble seemed to follow him everywhere, like a stray dog you once fed that won't go away no matter how many stones you throw at it. Despite his best efforts, his friends and mentors had died in his hands. His wife, the only woman he had really cared about, had died a horribly premature death, as had so many of the women he had loved. A string of mistresses, each more crass than the last one, made sure his end found him penniless near a dumpster, prematurely aged; a broken, friendless man.

In short, James had led a hard life. A life consisting of broken promises, death and countless tragedies, like pages from a madman's manuscript. That is why, as he drew his last breath, a thin smile of relief played on his chafed lips. He let go, and his spirit floated out of his body and into the cold night air. Finally free, he let himself forget his hardships and travails; to allow himself a glimmer of hope that things might finally change for the best.

His sight dimmed, as if a cloud of darkness had descended upon him, broken only by dancing flickers of light. Just before oblivion swallowed him, a thunderous applause filled his ears. Someone's voice boomed over the ovation, amplified by an invisible microphone:

"Thank you for watching James' Life with us tonight. And what a great life it was!"

The invisible crowd hooted and hollered in anticipation.

"This new 3D technology is great, isn't it, folks? How about we watch it again?" the voice thundered.

A sense of despair washed over everyone's favorite British spy as the projector's light shone on his life once again.

Infinite Waters

*S**he moaned in frustration. "That was too brief."*
I raised an eyebrow. "Was it?"
"Yes!"
With a theatrical flourish, I directed her gaze back to the pulsing, whirling light inside the ball.

Infinite Waters: 9+1 Speculative Fiction Short Stories

Two's a Crowd

"Can you believe that idiot?" I spat the words as soon as I slammed the car door shut.

"Honey, that idiot is your older brother." My wife looked at the mirror and patted her lips with her index finger. She opened her purse, oblivious to my rage.

"*Older* brother? He's, like, ten minutes older than me!"

Susan pressed her lipstick to her lips and ran it across them. Why was she bothering, anyway? We were alone in the car. Whom was she trying to impress? "Can we just go?" I said with a sigh. "My head hurts."

"Why did you have the red wine, then? You know it gives you a headache." She turned on the radio, obviously anticipating silence during the trip back home. After all, I never had much to say after our monthly dinners at my brother's. A recurrent affair that I had come to dread and hate with equal passion.

"What choice did I have? That's all they offered us."

"I'm sure they didn't do it on purpose." She wiggled her fingers and smiled at the couple waving at us from their door.

When she blew my brother a kiss, I leaned down and pretended not to notice them, absorbed by something on my shoe. *I probably just stepped on my turd of a brother.* The thought made me chuckle, then a thought killed my mirth. "You always support him." I did not care to hide my bitterness.

She checked the mirror and backed out of the gate. "That's not true."

"Sure it is. Sometimes I could swear that you like him better."

She threw me an annoyed glance. "Not this again."

Why not? He always stole whatever I had my eye on. Ever since we were children. My precious red ball. My silver bike. My first girlfriend. The bastard even took her to Lover's Hill in my *car. The car he stole from me. Why not you, too?* Yet, I knew better than to voice my angry thoughts.

As soon as we arrived home, I brushed my teeth and went straight to bed without a word. Susan took her sweet time getting ready, and I had nearly fallen asleep when she finally landed on the bed with all the grace of a drunken hippopotamus. "You wkmup," I mumbled.

"Sorry, dear." She applied some night cream to her face and rubbed her fingers vigorously as she gave me a quick peck on my cheek, then switched off the light on her nightstand.

I pretended to fall asleep right away, although in truth my mind was racing with murderous thoughts. I saw in my head his smirk when he announced he had renovated the beach house, and ground my teeth. The house—this was the last straw. The house that our parents had promised to me. The one that he had gotten through that joke of a will, magically produced out of our dead mother's drawer. The one I would have contested, but for the advice of my darling wife. *We already have a beach house,* she had argued. *Just think of all the extra cost. Not to mention the taxes!* I moaned and turned my back at her, furious at them both. *Why does everyone always support him?*

It is, perhaps, no surprise that I dreamed of my brother that night. I was standing in the middle of a lush field, a light wind ruffling my hair. The sun bathed my body in its soothing rays. Colorful flowers released their sweet aroma, filling the air with pleasant fragrances. I closed my eyes and took a deep breath to take it all in, when a dark cloud cut off the sunshine. I opened my eyes again and shot an annoyed look to the sky. My gaze caught on a sudden movement in the distance. A lone figure stood far away, hands on his hips. I squinted to see better. In a split second, the figure stood next to me. A spasm ran through my face.

"Hey, bro." My brother's lips twisted into a wide grin. Behind him, the beach house shimmered into existence, the white-washed walls flickering as if made of smoke.

My hands tightened into fists. Then a thought crossed my mind. I deliberately unclenched them and flashed him my sweetest smile. "Why don't you show me around?"

His brows knitted for a second, then we found ourselves in the living room. I was surprised by the changes to the house. He had spent half the evening describing the renovation, of course, but I had responded by drinking, in effect blocking him out. And yet here was the brand new staircase, with the polished silver maple banisters.

The elegant furniture. The white oak floors. Had he mentioned all this last night? Everything was the same, yet different. The place even smelled different to what I remembered. I traced the fragrance to a discreet device plugged into a wall socket and scrunched my nose.

From the corner of my eye, I saw a smirk on his face. "Like what I did with my place?"

Blood thumped on my temples, but I managed to hide my feelings behind a clenched grin. "Looks great." I had to get out of there before I punched him. Or worse. "Say, how 'bout I make us some coffee?" I slipped into the kitchen while my brother stood in the middle of the room, still smirking at the unnerving effect the renovation had on me.

The kitchen, too, was all different from the last time I had been to the old house. I leaned on the spotless counter until I cooled down enough to rummage through the cabinets. Inside one, I found a glass bowl filled with espresso capsules. I fished out two and made sure the machine had enough water before I switched it on.

A minute later, the machine groaned and the coffee's strong aroma filled my nostrils. I absent-mindedly opened a cabinet while waiting for the first cup to fill. My gaze fell on an orange plastic bottle, a black skull clearly visible on it. I picked it up, removed the lid and took a whiff. The pungent smell burned my nose and I recoiled. Then, on a whim, I dropped a few drops into the steaming cup.

I placed the bottle back into the cabinet before pouring the second cup, making sure I remembered which was which. Once I had both cups in my hand, I walked back out into the living room. My brother was sitting on a new, white leather couch, browsing on his tablet. I sat down beside him and handed him the first cup I had made.

"Watch it!" He took the cup with careful fingers and nodded towards the sofa. "You wouldn't believe how much this cost. Italian leather and all that."

I rolled my eyes and watched him take a sip, his gaze still fixed on the screen in his hands. His brow furrowed and he coughed.

"Strong," he said in a throaty voice. His gaze shot up from the tablet to meet mine. "Can you believe this?" He shoved the device into my hands. I pretended to read the news; something about an old friend of ours, who had lost his fortune in the dotcom bust. I couldn't care less, really. I waited for him to empty his cup.

A few minutes later, he made a pained grimace. "I'm not feeling well." He clutched his stomach. "Help me!"

I chortled, enjoying the sight of him emptying its contents onto his precious sofa, and shook my head as he collapsed onto the well-polished floor. *Serves you right.* I took a sip from my own cup and watched a funny cat video on the tablet. Meanwhile, his body quivered and spasmed, until he finally lay still.

A couple of videos later, a faraway sound invaded my serenity. It sounded like a phone, but I could not see one anywhere around. Then, the earth shook. *Earthquake!* I jumped to my feet.

"Yes?"

It took me a moment to figure out I had been dreaming. The earth was not shaking; that had been my wife, who had swiveled her feet off the bed in order to reach the phone on her nightstand. The mattress groaned under her shifting weight.

"What time is it?" I mumbled. Not really expecting an answer, I glanced through heavy lids at the clock on the nightstand. *Oh for goodness' sake, it's the middle of the night! Who the hell would call us at this hour?*

"Shh!" My wife waved at me with her left hand, her right one pressing the phone to her ear. "We'll be right there."

She hung up and turned to me, an agitated expression on her face. "It's your brother. He got sick after we left. They have him at the hospital."

"What?" I stopped rubbing the sleep from my eyes.

"Somehow, he got poisoned. We have to go." She did not even look at me as she dived into her closet. "And don't you dare start any of your—"

She stopped mid-sentence as I bolted out of bed and tore a fresh shirt from the hanger. *Did I cause this?*

Minutes later, I was already in the car, buttoning my shirt. I drummed my fingers on the steering wheel. *How is it possible?* When I could not take the waiting for Susan any longer, I honked. A moment later, she jumped into the car. "I'm coming, already! Stop honking—you'll wake everyone up!"

I stepped on the gas even as she was shutting her door. The car screeched in the night and sped down the empty roads.

Susan threw me a worried glance. "Can you even drive? You've had a lot to drink."

"I'm fine." *No, it couldn't have been me. Could it?*

We pulled up at the hospital and I raced out of the car and into a narrow corridor. "Where is he?" I cried out to a sleepy nurse behind a glass pane.

"Excuse me?"

My wife pushed me to the side. "We're looking for Mr. Thomas. They brought him in with food poisoning." I ran my fingers through my hair, touching more scalp than hair. *I have to tell her.*

"Susan, there's something—"

She threw me a distraught look. "Everything will be fine." She grabbed my hand and tugged. "This way." We hurried down a corridor and into an elevator. I tapped my foot, infuriated at the slow ride. My urge to share my dream with her had left me as suddenly as it had appeared. *She'll just think I'm crazy.* Four floors up, we heard a soft *ding* and the doors slid open.

Still holding my hand, she led me forward and into a barely-lit room. On a bed lay my brother. His wife was slumped on a chair next to him. She lifted her head when we entered. "Oh, hi, Susan!"

"Hi, Jill. How is he?" Her voice betrayed her worry.

"The doctors pumped his stomach. Whatever it was he drank, it was so acidic that it burned his throat on both the way down and up."

"How... how is that even possible?" I stammered.

She looked at me as she had just realized I was standing there. "No idea. He was fine when we went to bed. I swear, I did nothing." She sank her head into her palms and cried softly, while my wife sat down next to her and took her in her arms. Every now and then, she stole anxious looks at the still body on the bed.

Not you. Me.

The commotion caused my brother to open his eyes. His soft gaze wandered from the two women to me. When it reached my eyes, his face hardened. "What was in the coffee?" he rasped.

My mouth gaped. "I... What..."

His wife shot up and grabbed his hand. "The doctors said you shouldn't speak, darling. Try not to speak."

"The coffee," he said, his eyes dripping malice. "He put something in it."

"You didn't have any coffee last night, darling. You said it was too late. You had some scotch after dinner. Remember?"

His face scrunched up in puzzlement. "It's the drugs," his wife whispered. "He's confused."

I nodded, trying to ignore the thick drops of sweat trickling down my back. My brother closed his eyes and sank his head into the pillow with a soft sigh. Guilt overcame me. I staggered out of the room, holding onto the smooth wall for support. I replayed the dream in my head over and over again, struggling to make sense of it all.

"The doctor said he'll be fine."

I spun around and almost bumped into Susan. I forced a smile on my face. "Good."

She gave me a questioning look. "Are you okay? You look like you've seen a ghost."

You don't look too good yourself. "Just worried," I lied. Or perhaps it wasn't a lie. I *was* worried, just not about him.

She took me in her arms. "You're a good brother."

"Huh?"

"You act like you hate him, but when push comes to shove, you're there for him." She touched my cheek with gentle fingers. "I mean, look at how upset you are."

I noticed her ashen face as she said this. *We both are.* With a sigh, I took her hand and we made a beeline to the car. As soon as we returned home, I wasted no time going back to bed. Surprisingly enough, it did not take me long to fall asleep again. The minute my eyelids closed, I found myself inside the beach house again. With no one around, I looked around at my leisure. He had redone the fireplace as well. I traced the fine carvings on the Cipollino marble, admiring the smooth texture.

"I know it was you."

I jumped out of my skin when I heard my brother's voice behind me. I swirled around to face him. His face looked taut, with deep black circles under his sunken eyes. I forced a smile on my lips. "I'm glad you're feeling better."

"You bastard! You were here, then you gave me coffee. What did you put inside?"

"We're twins, remember? If I'm a bastard, so are you." I took a step back.

He came closer, raising his clenched fists. "You poisoned me, didn't you?"

"That's cold, bro. Real cold." I took another step back and my leg stumbled on something. A fire iron clanged onto the floor. I leaned down and grasped it, then shot back up, holding it in front of me. "Don't come any closer."

"Why not?" A wide, contemptuous grin appeared on his face. "This is my house. You're intruding."

Maybe if he hadn't had that stupid grin, I would not have done what I did. But all I could think about was wiping it off his face. I raised the iron and bashed his head with it. "*My* house," I bellowed as I pounded him with it. I ignored his scream of pain. "*My* girlfriend. *My* car. *My* wife. Mine! Mine!" With every word, I cracked the iron to his head.

I watched him on the floor. His eyes betrayed his surprise, but he no longer moved. Blood pooled under his head. I watched the pool grow, breathless.

From afar, the ringing resumed.

Next thing I remember, I was standing in the same hospital elevator with my wife. My whole body still shook with adrenaline as I darted into his room. My brother still lay on the bed, only now thick gauze covered the top of his head. A small part of it, wide as a quarter, was a deep red. *Right where I hit him.* His wife was crying softly next to him.

My wife ran towards Jill. "What happened?"

"I don't know. Some sort of seizure. The doctors said he's lucky to be alive."

"He bled inside his head, didn't he?" My voice sounded far away, as if the words belonged to someone else.

Jill threw me a surprised glance. "Yes, they called it a subdural hematoma." She wiped tears from her eyes with a crumbled tissue. "How did you know?"

I nodded towards the gauze. "I saw they opened up his skull to relieve the pressure." The whole situation felt unreal, like a nightmare. I kept expecting to wake up—only I could not. "How did it happen? Did he hit his head somewhere?"

"No! He just screamed. I could not wake him up." Her tears started flowing more freely now. "The doctors said he could have died," she said between loud wails.

I gave her shoulder a squeeze. "We're here now. Whatever you need, just let us know."

A pang of guilt shot through my heart when she reached and grabbed my hand. "Thank you."

It was almost dawn by the time we left. We said nothing on the way home. When we arrived, my wife opened the door to climb out of the car, then paused. "What a night." A faint smile broke through her lips. "But I'm proud of you."

I wanted to cackle and cry and scream—all at the same time. Instead, I pushed my lips into an exhausted smile. "Let's try and get some rest, shall we?"

"Now?" She nodded towards the sky. In the east, the first rays of the sun chased away the night, forming deep pink and purple bands. "I don't think I can sleep."

"I'm beat." I wasn't lying. My limbs felt leaden. Mixed feelings filled me; feelings I could not admit even to myself. Every now and then, guilt and sorrow strangled the glee, then the joy returned. It all numbed my thoughts. I just wanted to crawl under the duvet and forget this night ever happened. Pretend that I had not almost killed my brother.

But how could it be? How could I be responsible for his condition? I knew it was a mistake. I could not have hurt him. Part of me wanted to, for sure. But I was no monster. And even if I were, how? It was impossible. It was divine justice; had to be. He was being punished for everything he had stolen from me over all these years.

"I'll call the office and let them know you won't be going in today. You just stay in bed and get some rest."

"Thank you." I loved it when she took care of me like that. It made me feel warm; protected.

To be honest, I did not expect to fall asleep. I thought I would toss and turn for an hour or two, then get up. Instead, I sank almost immediately into a deep slumber. And I had another dream. As before, the setting was the beach house's living room. The fire iron was tossed to the floor in front of the fireplace, next to a large crimson pool. Countless dots stained the white floorboards and the marble. I leaned closer and dabbed a finger into the scarlet pool. Its edges had turned a rusty brown; the color of caked blood. The center was still bright red. And wet.

A deep, rumbling thunder warned me of an impending storm. I left the quiet of the house to step out onto the verandah. It overlooked a squally sea that crashed against the cliffs below. A gust of wind streamed over me, whipping my face with tiny droplets. Moments later, heavy clouds released sheets of rain. Churning winds ripped across the rocks, howling through the rocky crevices. And yet, I did not move. Even when I saw him.

He approached me from the sea, walking through the air, as if the storm itself was bearing him. My darling brother. His eyes were gleaming like ambers made of fire. When he spotted me, he sped up. There was no qualm in his stride; no hesitation. Only blistering determination. When he approached, he lunged at me without warning. I grabbed his shirt. Using his momentum, I twirled him around, then released him. He crashed against the wall. Screaming with fury, he came at me once more. I tried to grab him again, but he ducked under my hands. His arms clenched around my waist. His shoulder knocked the wind out from my lungs. We crashed down the stairs.

I cried out in frustration and smacked his head with my fists. He refused to let go, pushing me farther down the narrow path that led through the gardens and to the sea. I managed to get my arms under his and thrust upwards. This finally broke his grip on me. We circled each other, both breathless. Our movement brought us closer to the fence. He swiped his arm to punch my face. I bent my body backwards. His fist split the air above me. Without pausing, he swirled around, lowering his body at the same time. He continued his spinning motion, this time aiming at my legs. I dropped and rolled to my side, jumping back on my feet almost immediately.

We glared at each other for a moment. The rain now fell in torrents. "That's the best you can do?" I taunted him. Bolts of lightning flashed in the sky.

"I hate you!" he screamed.

"You stole everything from me!" I yelled back at him. Thunder boomed all around us.

He smirked. "Including your wife. But you did nothing. You know why? 'Cause you're a loser. You'll *always* be a loser."

"No!" I lunged at him. He tried to sidestep me, but I was faster. We crashed against the wooden fence and dropped on the ground behind it, close to the cliff's edge. I raised myself to my feet and glared at him. "You've always taken everything from me. No more. I'll kill you."

"No, little brother. *I'll* kill you."

We both screamed and charged each other at the same time. Our hands clutched each other's throats. We squeezed the life out of each other, too caught up in our rage to notice that our thrashing about had brought us right to the edge. We continued strangling each other even as we dropped into the sea, where sharp rocks shred our bodies apart.

###

"I still can't believe it," Jill said. "You know, I always thought they hated each other."

Susan reached over and gave her hand a light squeeze. "So did I." They shared an awkward smile, stifling their tears. In front of them, people laid wreath upon wreath in front of two identical mahogany caskets. "But for them to die like that, at the very same time… the very same night… What could that mean?"

"That they loved each other very much. So much so, that they couldn't bear the thought of living without one another." Jill blew her nose softly into a tissue. "What else could it possibly mean?"

Infinite Waters: 9+1 Speculative Fiction Short Stories

Infinite Waters

She broke the contact with the sphere and sank back into her chair, panting. "That was... intense."

"Are you sure you want to continue?"

She smacked her lips. "Is there any water?"

I reached over to a small carafe and filled her a glass. She emptied it in three large gulps, then plonked it on the table with a satisfied ah!

"I'm ready. Show me more."

I pressed my lips together and tapped the table with my fingers. She placed her hand on mine, silencing the motion. "Please?"

Infinite Waters: 9+1 Speculative Fiction Short Stories

What's in a Name?

"That's an unusual name for a ship."

The man facing me across the table pulled the fat cigar from his lips, leaving it to simmer inside a round ashtray. Smoking is strictly prohibited on a spaceship, but if you are the ship's owner I guess normal rules do not apply. His thick brows met in the middle, as if pondering my words. Why, I could not fathom — surely, this was the single most usual comment he heard? His jowls quivered as he pushed his chair away to stand up. Hoisting his trousers up, he adjusted his lifejacket and grimaced, as if in pain.

"It was a bet." With a dismissive wave of his hand, he motioned me to follow him. "A stupid bet." He sighed as he ran his fingers through thinning hair. "I lost."

That much is obvious. "Are we going somewhere?" I asked politely and stood up. My recorder floated from the table to hover above us.

"I just want to show you around. I assume your viewers will want to know about the ship?"

I nodded my thanks. We weaved our way out of the smoke room and into the promenade deck. Reserved for the first-class passengers, this was not my usual kind of accommodations. My initial enthusiasm at finding out I had been sent on an assignment that allowed me to spend a week on a cruise around the moon had waned as soon as I heard the details. The lush accommodations, however, made me rethink my initial apprehension.

The ship owner led me into the wide corridor crossing the deck. I snuck a look into a gym room, filled with ripped people in sweatpants admiring their visage in full-wall mirrors. Strangely enough, the lifejackets did not seem to bother them. A smiling blonde at the reception was handing a towel and a lifejacket to a man dressed from top to bottom in grey flannel. Splashing was heard from a wide, steel-framed door behind her. I guessed the sounds came from an indoor swimming pool. Judging by the steam on the glass, the doors next to it led to a spa or sauna. My muscles ached for a massage, but that would have to wait. I was here for a job.

"Do they wear lifejackets in the pool?" I wondered aloud. I guessed that an inflatable nanosuit that could keep you alive for an hour in space would probably be waterproof, but it still seemed strange.

"Everyone has to wear their lifejacket twenty-four-seven. It's part of the insurance policy." For the first time since we met, the foreboding cloud lifted from his eyes and the man grinned. "It gives them something to tell their friends after the cruise."

"Is the name also why you only do moon cruises, instead of Mars ones? To avoid any stray comets?"

"Can't be too careful," the man agreed.

I stepped aside as a slender girl rushed out a door and almost crashed on us. She was balancing half a dozen e-books and tablets, taken from what I guessed was the lending library. With a shy smile, she dashed down the corridor and into the reading room. Her lifejacket bounced against the doorframe, almost making her drop the devices, but she managed to hold on to them at the last moment.

"Are you coming?"

Despite his short stature and rotund figure, the ship owner could move fast. I hurried up after him, my eye catching on the Renaissance-style trimmings. The decoration was worthy of a floating five-star hotel. All first-class common rooms were adorned with ornate wood paneling and expensive furniture instead of the practical simplicity usually found on spaceships.

We passed an open door leading to the outside deck. In a few hours, this would be filled with a throng of passengers socializing, promenading or relaxing in hired deck chairs and sculpted wooden benches. An artificial sun would be shining on the dome covering the ship. Now, however, the deck lay empty, much like the space surrounding us. I stole a look outside. The vast emptiness of space caught my breath. Countless stars sparkled brighter than anything I had ever seen back on Earth. Our movement was so smooth, that it felt like sailing on a quiet pond. I half-expected a flock of wild geese to land on the deck at any moment.

Someone closed the door and passed me by, snapping me back to the present. I followed the ship owner down the Grand Staircase, one of the most distinctive features of the ship. It descended through seven decks. A dome of wrought iron and glass capping it admitted the artificial sunlight in the morning, although it now lay dark, like a black, polished diamond. A large, carved wooden panel above us contained a clock, with figures of "Honour and Glory crowning Time" flanking the clock face. I could not help but gape at the beauty of it all.

Upon reaching the landing, we entered an ornate hall lit by gold-plated light fixtures. Well-laid tables filled the room. White linen covered the tops. Silver cutlery clanked against porcelain dishes. Waiters meandered skillfully to serve dinner to hungry first-class passengers.

Music came from the far end, obscuring the diners' soft murmur. I recognized "O mio Babbino Caro" and half-expected to hear a soprano — maybe even Callas herself, brought back from the dead — singing the aria. "The Café Parisien offers the best French haute cuisine for first-class passengers," the man said with a well-practiced flourish.

"And the music?"

"Our very own small *ensemble*. Eight musicians, the very best."

"They'd have to be, to play with their lifejackets on," I could not help but joke.

He did not seem to share my mirth, and muttered something under his breath. He spun around to continue the tour, when a jolt reverberated through the hull. It was so strong that it knocked me off my feet, sending me to land on my lifejacket. A mannequin crashed through a glass display and dropped next to me. *I survived a cruise on…* , the t-shirt it wore read. The rest of the inscription was obscured by the doll's broken arm.

I heard shouts all around me. Angry claxons blared in alarm. People clamored. Lights dimmed, and shone again. Then, it all stopped. An eerie silence fell. Dazed people struggled to get their bearings. Expensive leather shoes and elegant high heels stepped on salmon and pheasant as stunned diners rose to their feet. Fear and silent pleas for help filled the passengers' eyes. I turned to the ship owner, but he had disappeared. From afar, I heard one long continuous wailing hiss, like locusts on a midsummer night in the woods. *Are we decompressing?* I decided to follow the noise. The flickering lights allowed me to reach the nearest exit, pushing through the nervous throng.

I had just reached the door handle when the floor tilted. The vessel reared up, followed by a rumbling roar and a muffled explosion. I pushed through the door and grabbed the railing. Above me, the dome cracked. A small chunk flew away, blown out by the pressure. My eyes gaped at the ugly sight. A second piece followed. The ship let out a terrible groan and quivered, like a mongrel trying to throw the fleas off its back. *Crack!* The dome split open with a deafening blast. Deck chairs and sculpted wooden benches flew around me to burst through the fracture. The clamor drowned out my scream.

The gushing atmosphere sucked me upwards. The shock took the breath out of my lungs. I flew towards the dome at an increasing speed, gasping for air. The lifejacket sprang to life. Nanocarbon blades clasped and banded together to form an impenetrable barrier that covered me from head to toe. Air hissed in my ears. After a heart-stopping moment of weightlessness, I crashed against the dome and yelled in pain. My hands grabbed the dome's torn edge. I held on for a moment, my feet already dangling in space. I started sliding, carried away by the rushing air. My eyes searched in vain for anything to hold on to. Then, I let go.

I popped through the gap in the dome, like a cork. I drifted away from the safety of the spaceship and into the endless void of space. I flailed my arms and legs to stop the dizzying motion. My heart beat so fast, I thought it would pop out of my chest. Finally, it occurred to me to let my lifejacket guide me to safety. Valves hissed and the mad rotation stopped, just as I was about to hurl my stomach's contents against my mask.

Something banged against me. I spun around, startled, and came up against a lifeboat. An airlock opened up silently before me. Too exhausted to haul myself, I let the men already inside pull me inside.

The door behind me closed in silence. Air hissed into the airlock. My ears popped as sound returned. I punched the clasp deactivating the lifejacket. With a soft clicking sound, it retracted back into my belt, ready to spring back to life at a moment's notice. I landed on the metal floor, still nauseated. It smelled of engine oil, petrol and ozone. The sweetest smell to ever hit my nostrils. Someone helped me to my feet and sat me down. I nodded my thanks and coughed to clear my lungs. Tears burned my eyes and my throat.

"Are you all right?"

Recognizing the voice, I looked up and saw the ship owner. "I will be, thanks," I rasped after a moment. I drew a deep breath, grateful to be alive. "What the hell happened?"

"A ship collided with us," the man said. "Those idiots must have been drunk or something."

I shook my head. I had heard stories of crews drinking on the job, but this was one for the books. The huge cruise ship was not exactly hard to miss.

I glanced outside. The dome had now disappeared. Silent explosions dotted the ship's hull. Numerous lifeboats shot out of gaping holes in the decks. A second spaceship tilted drunkenly next to it. In the darkness of space, it was hard to make out, but it looked like a freighter.

My eye caught on something like countless heads bobbing around is. "My God," I whispered. "Are those people?"

The man leaned next to me and craned his head to look. "No, that's not heads." He looked forlorn. "It's lettuce. Frozen lettuce. That damn ship was filled with it. Probably for the moon colonies." His eyes glinted with something akin to madness. "We were struck by a freighter carrying iceberg lettuce."

"Iceberg lett—" I coughed to swallow the mad cackle that rose to my throat, shaking my head. "Buddy, *that's* why you don't call your ship the Titanic II."

Infinite Waters

She burst into laughter. "Good one!"

I shrugged. I've seen the stories before. I reach for the ball. "If that's—"

Her head jerked towards me. "More!" Without waiting for me to speak, she shoved away my hands, and stared into the globe.

Infinite Waters: 9+1 Speculative Fiction Short Stories

The Lucky Bastard

The low-lit bunker was as quiet as a grave. The kind of grave the entire world would be like, if I didn't stop the upcoming apocalypse. I glanced at the stony-faced people in the room. Uniforms of all shapes and colors surrounded me. A clean-shaven aide pushed a briefcase onto the table. His hands shook with a slight tremor as he popped the lid open. The insides contained a screen and a compact keyboard. He tapped it and the screen flickered to life with a soft *beep*. I inserted the crescent key hanging from my neck into a silver slot, while the aide took a respectful step back.

A man with as many golden stars on his lapels as the fingers on both my hands produced a similar key and pushed it into a second slot. Our gazes met for a moment. I nodded. We both turned the keys slowly until a soft *click* confirmed the system was now armed. Behind me, the entire wall lit up, mirroring the small screen facing me. I felt nothing. No emotion, no fear, no hope.

Is this what destiny had in mind all along? To hang the fate of the entire world on me?

Destiny. Fate. Luck. Whatever you called it, I was intimately familiar with it. 'The Lucky Bastard,' the papers called me; friends and foes alike. Little did they know just how accurate that was.

I never knew my father. Probably some loser my drug-addled mother met on the streets. She died within minutes of delivering me. My luck kicked in right away. I stole the heart of the doctor who delivered me. He and his wife had been trying for years, with no success. He later said I was the perfect child for them. He knew the minute he laid his eyes on me.

With no known relatives, the adoption went through right away. My parents lavished me with all their love and attention, the way only adoptive parents can. All I had to do was ask for something and it was mine. I didn't let them down, either. Luck had gifted me with unusually spacious lungs and a unique metabolism. I won one competition after another. A string of athletic scholarships let me skim through school. As long as I could remember where and when the race took place, all I had to do was show up and the win was mine. I won my first Olympics barely out of high school. Didn't even have to train.

Universities fought over me. My second Olympics, I won while studying management at a prestigious Ivy League university. Although studying may be too strong a word. I didn't even have to show up at class. At the finals, I was sure I would fail. Luck saved me again. A computer glitch somehow caused my test to disappear. Eager to avoid embarrassment, the department offered me my degree without so much as a peep.

I lacked for nothing. Money, fame, women; all mine for the taking. Especially the women. They fawned over my proverbial chiseled jaw, my sparkling blue eyes, and my mane of thick, black hair. Plus, I was an Ivy League -trained manager on top of being an Olympic-winning athlete. A jock with a brain. Who could resist that? I had a different girl in my arms each night. I never committed to anyone, of course. Why would I? The moment one brief relationship was over, a dozen more were beckoning.

Some took it harder than others. My only long-term relationship—two and a half months—committed suicide over me. Stupid bitch. Luckily, her best friend also had a crush on me. She spoke to the press of the girl's depression. Again and again. I still wonder how much of it was true. Regardless, in the end, I came out as a martyr. Instead of dragging me down, my stock had never been higher.

The publicity attracted the attention of a head hunter. She tracked me down and invited me to one of the best law firms in the country. I was to start low, but as luck would have it, the owner had just lost his son. Not only were we the same age, but he had been the spitting image of me. When I entered the man's office for the first time, his bloodshot eyes widened as if he had seen a ghost.

It took me less than a year to make Junior Partner. Within five, I was Senior Partner, then, when the old man died, he left me the company and everything he owned.

Some grumbled, of course, but soon afterwards, a local politician was impeached. He swiftly became our largest client. The money he poured into the office put a stop to any complaints. And when we saved his skin on a technicality, he introduced me to his party leaders.

A couple of years later, he died of a Viagra and coke-induced heart attack in the arms of his mistress. I made sure none of it reached the papers. In gratitude, the party nominated me for his seat. Naturally, I won. My track record—both figuratively and literally—did all the work for me, really. Once again, all I had to do was show up and the spoils were there for the taking.

The only thing my record was not good for was the presidency. Not having a wife, three point five children and a cute dog does that. I was good enough for vice president, though. And when a crazy bastard shot the president, barely a year into his term, I found myself at the top of the world. POTUS by default.

I barely had time to enjoy it, though. My predecessor had poked the Bear once too often, and now the Bear just poked back. With nukes. Or so our sensors told us.

"Mister President? The code?"

The general's voice snapped me out of my reverie. It had a hint of a quaver. I could hardly blame him. I stared at the screen in front of me. My finger hovered over the keyboard. All I had to do was punch in the codes that would activate our defense grid. Powerful lasers and a barrage of missiles would take out the nukes fast approaching the East Coast within seconds.

The Russkies knew this. Hell, they depended on it. They didn't want an apocalypse any more than we did. They only shot their missiles as a warning, knowing we would shoot them down. It was just their way of growling, "Back off." So, why had I not entered the command yet?

Dozens of tiny dots raced on the screen. I squinted to see them better. Red pixels edged towards the green line separating land from the sea. They would cross over at any moment now.

A smile tugged at the corner of my lips. What if I let them through? Maybe they carried nukes. Maybe not. My heart drummed in my chest. Was this excitement? It'd been so long that I couldn't even recognize the feeling. My pulse quickened. If we were nuked, even my cursed luck wouldn't be able to save me from a life of toil and struggle—would it?

All my life, Luck took care of me, and I loathed her for it. Never struggled, never strived. I couldn't remember the last time I'd enjoyed something. My food had no flavor. Sex was a chore. Music had no melody. My life was reduced to satisfying one pathetic need after another. The highlight of the day was my morning piss.

My finger still hovered over the buttons. Then again, perhaps I didn't make it. Maybe even the half-mile separating us from the surface was not enough in case of a direct hit. I shrugged. If I died, then this cursed life of immeasurable blandness would be over. I could see no downside.

"Mister President?" The quaver in the general's voice was palpable now. He bit his lower lip. His fingers twitched towards the briefcase. His gaze shot between the wall screen and my face.

I glanced at the bug-eyed people staring at me from across the table. *Beep beep beep.* A warning. The red dots had just crossed over the green border. My smile grew into a grin as I snapped the lid shut. "Feeling lucky, gentlemen?"

Infinite Waters

"*Son of a...*" *She leaned back and shut her eyes, drawing in sharp breaths.*

I reached and placed my hand over hers. "Are you all right?"

She nodded, then opened her eyes wide and stared back into the misty shapes. "Ready."

"Perhaps you'd like to—" I started to say.

"Shh!"

Infinite Waters: 9+1 Speculative Fiction Short Stories

A Twist of the Tail

Despite the early hour, I was covered in sweat. The day promised to be another scorcher. It *was* August, after all. I let out a small groan and faced the cloudless sky, grateful for a brief whiff of morning breeze, before I grabbed the suitcase's handle again. *What have I put inside, anyway?* My mind was foggy and my head heavy, like the luggage in my hands. One of its plastic wheels squeaked in protest as I tugged, to remind me that it was made to travel on the flat surface of an airport; not on a street's gravel.

Where was I, anyway? Nothing looked familiar in this small town. I knew I was only passing through, but still, it couldn't be that different to every other town I'd seen on my journey. Or could it? I felt like a salmon navigating the currents of infinite waters to reach an unknown destination. I shook my head in a vain attempt to clear it. I was trying to piece together my memories, but it was like working on a puzzle that was missing half its pieces.

A portly man emerged from a grocery store. "Morning, Jill!"

Who's Jill? I ignored him and fixed my gaze to the bus stop ahead. The suitcase bumped over a large pebble and almost tipped over. I hastened to steady it with my other hand. My tail twisted in irritation.

Wait, what? I let go of the handle and touched the bump on my lower back, just above the place where my body split into a shallow crack. There was a small protrusion there, twitching left and right. *Huh. That's a new one.* I felt sure I should be worried about it, yet I shrugged it off. *Perhaps it's just my imagination. I have to visit a bathroom later, to see what's really there.*

"Everything all right?"

The grocer waved at me and my hand snapped back to the suitcase's handle. I forced a smile on my lips. *No, it's not! I don't know you, I've got some sort of protrusion growing out of my butt and I have no idea where the heck I am.* "Never better, thank you."

His white moustache twitched under thick lips. He smiled back at me and nodded, making his crimson jowls shake like cherry-flavored jello. "Need any help?"

"I'm good, thanks." I looked away, tugging once again at the suitcase's handle. *People are strange when you're a stranger*, a voice sang in my head. I couldn't wait to get away from this strange town. Or was it just me who was weird?

My gaze caught on a dog licking himself clean at the grocer's feet. He stopped to stare at me, one leg stuck in the air as if warming up for a dance recital. He was a scruffy, brown thing, with white patches and twitching whiskers like those of his owner. The sight triggered conflicting emotions within me. *I like dogs, don't I? Or am I afraid of them?* Something stirred in my mind, but disappeared as soon as I tried to grasp it, leaving me frustrated, as if trying to grab smoke with my fingers.

The mutt stretched lazily, then made a beeline towards me. I froze and let him approach. He sniffed my leg, first almost absent-mindedly, then with ever increasing urgency. As soon as his nose reached my behind, he let out a surprised yelp and dashed off to cower between the grocer's legs. His neck hair was standing up, making him look like a tiny dinosaur. A strange sound, like a growl interspersed with plaintive yelps, was coming from his throat.

The grocer knelt to comfort the dog. "What's the matter, boy? It's just Jill."

I ignored the man's surprised stare and finally reached the bus stop. I crashed on the chipped wooden bench that sat under its rusty roof. With a loud sigh, I let go of the suitcase and checked my hands. They shook from the effort and felt numb. I rubbed my palms against my forearms to start the blood circulating again. When the feeling returned to my fingers, I closed my eyes and leaned backwards, resting my head against the bus stop's glass pane.

"Jill?"

My eyes flew open. The voice sounded vaguely familiar. It cut through my mind's fog like a foghorn. Two soft, green eyes met my confused gaze. A handsome face hovered over mine, worry etched on it. A name emerged from somewhere within the oblivion of my soul. "Henry?"

Relief shone in his eyes. "Hey, honey! What are you doing?"

His gentle features set off memories, each dragging the other into my consciousness like a string of pearls. Our meeting, at the grocer's, thirty years ago. I had just arrived to the small town, from... I couldn't remember where from, but it mattered little. Memories flooded me now; our brief, yet intense courtship. Our wedding. Our first dog, then our second one. The birth of our children. My hand shot down involuntarily and clutched my belly, as if tracing the stretch marks hiding under the loose skirt.

I remembered our first house, a tiny apartment that we filled with our love. Then our second one, the one with the large garden. The one where our children grew up, before heading off to the world. How could I have forgotten it all?

"What happened?" I whispered the words and grasped the handle of my suitcase, in a desperate attempt to unite the two worlds; the elusive one in my head and the physical one surrounding me.

"When I woke up, you had left. Mister Stevens called to say he had seen you at the bus stop, and that you looked confused."

Mister Stevens. The grocer. Of course.

"So, I came to find you." Henry sat down next to me and I scooted over to give him more space. He moved even closer and took my hand into his, his slender fingers hot on my skin. "What's wrong, darling?"

My eyes misted. "I... I'm not sure. I don't remember much. Just that I woke up and I had to go..." My mind struggled to remember, but the memory of this morning had already melted away, like dew disappearing from the leaves under the morning sun, leaving them dry as bones. I shook my head. "I don't know."

"How is she?"

I spun around to face an elderly man.

"Hey, Doc," Henry said and stood up. "She seems fine now."

The newcomer sat next to me, on the other side of the bench, and I swallowed nervously. "I'm fine, really."

He stared deep into my eyes. "Do you know who I am?"

I smiled. Of course I knew him. The town's physician had been to our house more times than I cared to remember. This being such a small town, he doubled as pediatrician, and he had put in many a midnight call as our children were growing up. I took his hand and a smile tugged at my lips. "How could I forget?"

He mirrored my smile and lifted a finger into the air. "Can you follow my finger?"

I did as instructed. After a cursory examination, he patted my hand. "You seem fine. Perhaps you bumped your head somewhere?"

I laughed at that; everyone knew what a klutz I was. "Don't I always?" I then turned to Henry. "Can we go home?"

He cocked his head at Doc, a silent question in his eyes.

Doc cleared his throat. "I don't see why not. Just spend some time in bed and get some rest. I'll drop by tomorrow to see how you're doing."

"Thanks, Doc." I raised myself and nodded my appreciation.

Henry stood up after me and kissed my forehead. "Come on, honey. Let's go home." He tugged at my suitcase. "Jesus, what have you put in here? Rocks?" He chuckled at his joke and started on his way towards home.

I stared at him for a moment, lost in sudden uncertainty. My hand traced my back with anxious fingers. There was nothing there. I sighed in relief and a wide grin pulled at my lips as a huge wave of love filled my soul. I must have been more confused than I realized. *I mean, a tail, of all things? Seriously?*

I let out an embarrassed chuckle. "Can you believe I can't even remember? We'll open it at home and find out."

As soon as the words left my mouth, I knew I have to stop him from opening the suitcase, but had no idea why. Or how. I was not worried, though. I'd think of something to take his mind off the suitcase once we're home. It would be just like that weekend when I had crashed his brand new car. We had spent an entire weekend in bed, while the town's mechanic worked overtime to have it ready by Sunday evening. Henry had not even found out about it until two weeks later, when he had finally noticed a scratch on the hood, and I had come clean. My punishment had been to spend another weekend in bed. Not too bad.

A mischievous grin tugged at my lips at the possibilities. After all, I had to spend some time in bed. Doctor's orders and all that. He laughed as I rushed towards him and took him by the arm, squishing my face against his shoulder.

###

The door's soft swish interrupted the low hum of the suborbital engines; the only other sound in the spacious bridge. A wide screen showed the green and blue planet rotating gently under the hidden spaceship.

"Yes?" The captain's hands were firmly clasped behind his back, but his stubby tail twitched back and forth, betraying his impatience. Staying too long over a planet with a space-faring civilization was always a risk. The ship might be invisible to most instruments, but there were people in orbit. People with eyes and cameras. And the slow progress of the evacuation meant that they had already stayed longer than originally planned.

The First Mate approached him, tapping a hand-held screen. "Of the one hundred and thirty Surrogates, eighteen have died in the past thirty years. One hundred and eleven are now on board. And one..." He swallowed nervously. "One is unaccounted for."

The captain spun around to face him, one eyebrow arched. "What do you mean, unaccounted?"

"We sent the signal. She acknowledged it and indicated she would collect all surveillance equipment and proceed to the rendezvous point. Then..." He hesitated for a moment and ran his fingers through his hair.

"Then, what?" the captain barked.

"We... we don't know. Her vitals are strong, but she never made it." The First Mate pressed his lips together. "What shall we do? Do we send someone after her?"

The captain tapped his index finger against his chin, lost in thought. "Could she have reverted to her Surrogate status?"

"It's rare, but it happens."

"What about her physiology? Is there anything..."

The First Mate shook his head. "Shouldn't be. Once the Surrogate persona takes over, she's all human again."

A flash on the screen drew the captain's attention. A silver spot over the atmosphere reflected the sun's light, like a tiny star. After a moment, it disappeared. "Their space station. That's it. We're out of time." He straightened his uniform with long, nervous strokes. "How long before we're back?"

"We'll pick up the new group of Surrogates in thirty years."

The captain tightened his jaw in determination. "We'll find her then. Prepare to jump."

The First Mate's fingers danced on the handheld screen. The soft hum changed pitch and volume as the massive jump engines sprang to life. "Very well, sir." He stole a look at the planet below them. It looked serene under the rising sun, like a beautiful green and blue marble. Somewhere down there, a woman just got a thirty-year extension to her undercover mission on Earth. "Have a lovely life, Mrs. Jones."

Infinite Waters

"So... Mrs. Jones..."

"Yep."

She leaned back and stared at the ceiling for a few moments. Then, she rested her arms on the table and fixed her gaze into the swirling shapes inside the globe. "Give me another."

"I'm not sure—"

"Just do it!"

Infinite Waters: 9+1 Speculative Fiction Short Stories

Is There a Doctor in the House?

"**M**iss Dominique?"

A girl with a blond ponytail and a bored look on her cute face lifted her hand. "No chewing gum in the classroom, Miss Dominique," I murmured absent-mindedly as I placed a neat tick mark next to her name.

The girl rolled her eyes in a theatrical manner. She pulled out a tissue from her bag and carefully spat into it. With a flick of her wrist and a giggle, she sent it flying. It landed on the hair of the boy sitting in front of her, like a slightly wet missile that homed in on its target. "Miss Dominique!" I tried to sound stern.

"Sorry," she mumbled and winked at the girl sitting next to her. They stifled their giggles under my glare.

I checked the boy sitting in front of them, but he seemed oblivious of the whole incident. He ran nervous fingers through his hair, tousling them further. When his fingers caught the tissue, he stared at it with curiosity, then tossed it aside. His gaze then lifted back outside, where dark clouds were gathering fast, before checking his watch.

No wonder they pick on him. It was not just that he was a foreigner. I tried to remember where he was originally from, but the name eluded me. Somewhere in Eastern Europe. The kid spoke with a funny accent that made it even harder for the other children to like him. I had heard that his family was very rich and powerful over there, but had been forced to leave during some kind of revolt or other. They had now come here for a new start.

I swallowed a sigh. I just wished the kid did a better job at fitting in. His faraway look was one problem, exacerbated by his thick, round glasses. His long, tousled hair made him look untidy, in a prep school classroom filled with smartly-dressed children. Then, the strange things he mumbled on constantly. His *experiments*, as he called them. That was how he always got in trouble. As for that white lab coat he was always sporting... *I'll bet that doesn't help with the bullying, either.*

Still, perhaps I should cut the kid some slack. Losing your home and friends and moving across half the world to a new place couldn't be easy. Plus, he had just lost his best friend. My gaze flicked over to the empty seat beside him. Ihor; the only other boy in the classroom who'd hang out with him. Probably because they both came from the same neck of the woods. A fine pair of misfits, those two. If only that boy had let go of the string before the lightning struck. Then again, what were they thinking, flying a kite during a storm? It was the new kid's idea, for sure. Another of his experiments, no doubt.

I noticed some questioning looks, so I cleared my throat and returned to the list in my hands. *Ihor Azarov.* I pursed my lips for a moment, then moved on to the next name. "Miss Foyle?"

"Here," came the bored reply. Outside, a thunder rumbled from afar.

"You forgot Ihor."

My gaze shot at the new kid. Children chuckled, but he ignored them.

"Excuse me?"

"You forgot Ihor," the kid repeated.

He stared right at me and our eyes locked. I opened my mouth to speak, but I wasn't sure what to say. I closed it again. A lightning bolt lit up the room. Its momentary flash made me realize just how dark the room had gotten. *That's quite a storm that's gathering. Maybe it's for the best. That way, they won't pick on the kid during the break.*

I lowered my gaze back to the list. "Mister Harry?"

"You forgot Ihor," the kid said for a third time.

A deep frown creased my forehead as I lifted my gaze at the little miscreant again. *Relax. He's probably just hurting. It's only denial. First stage of grief and all that, right?* My fingers drummed a nervous beat on the table.

A loud thunder crashed just outside the classroom. I jumped startled. "Ihor's dead," I blurted out. My voice sounded angrier than I expected.

"My dad says—"

Another bolt of lightning interrupted him. A bulb exploded overhead. Dominique let out a surprised yelp. Tiny glass shards flew to the floor.

"He says what?" I stared at the kid, daring him to continue. His face looked taut, tired; yet a look of triumph burned deep in the boy's sunken eyes.

Strange noises came from the corridor, like heavy footsteps. Thump, shuffle. Thump, shuffle. *What is that noise?* I threw the list onto the table and slammed my hand on the hard wood. "That is enough. What are you up to this time?"

As the doorknob rattled, a wide grin appeared on the kid's face.

"I asked you a question!"

Instead of an answer, the grin just got wider and he stared at the door. Another bolt of lightning silhouetted a hulking figure outside the glass pane. I jumped out of my seat and threw the door open. In the corridor, the school porter was pulling on a heavy crate. "Sorry, Professor, didn't mean to interrupt." A second porter ran to join him. The two of them heaved the crate together.

The boy's expression turned to one of dismay. He flicked his fingers, mumbling something. I shuffled over to his seat and leaned closer to make sense of his murmur. A strange sound—a cross between a moan and a groan—came from the doorway. The shuffling sound resumed on the hallway. *What are those idiots out there doing now?*

Behind the boy, Miss Dominique pushed her fist into her mouth to stifle a scream. The boy craned his head to look behind me. His gaze fell on the doorway. His face lit up like a kid who just got a chocolate bicycle for Christmas.

I let out an exasperated sigh and shook my head. "That's it, Mister Frankenstein. Tomorrow, I want to see you with your father."

Infinite Waters

*A*s soon as she jerked her gaze from the sphere, I draped it with its cover once again. "That was the last one," I said, my voice firm.

She snapped her head up to face me. "Why?"

"How much more inspiration can you want?" I asked and chuckled.

She gave me a daring look. "You don't know much about authors, do you?"

I lifted my shoulder in a half shrug. "Can't say I do."

"One more. Then I'll stop. Promise."

I studied her pleading face for a moment, then pulled the cover with a soft sigh.

Infinite Waters: 9+1 Speculative Fiction Short Stories

Sex and Dinner

"How about sex *and* dinner?" she asked, her throaty voice sending tingles to play on the fine hairs on his neck. She rubbed one fine, slender foot on her lengthy leg, to stress her point.

Her audacity caught his breath. They hardly knew each other, having met only a few minutes earlier. And yet here she was, her naked flesh provoking him into a frenzy. There was no mistaking the hunger in her eyes; the need for his body; her desire for his flesh.

He swallowed and tried to look away, to avoid her burning stare. She snickered at his discomfort as he lowered his eyes to examine his trembling fingers. *Speak! Say something!* His mouth obeyed the mental command and opened, but words failed him. His gaze caressed her nude body to linger once more on trim legs that seemed to go on forever. He bit his lip, his heart skipping a beat. She had him now; he would stop at nothing to slither between her mounds, to experience the ecstasy promised by her inviting, crooked smile; consequences be damned.

His determination slipped fast. With the last remnants of his strength, he made a final, desperate attempt to negotiate. To save himself. "Why not dinner first?" he croaked, a thick bead of sweat trickling down his forehead.

Her raspy laugh made his knees tremble. He leaned against a tree to stop himself from shaking. A delightful, mortified shiver travelled through his body and onto the wrinkled bark at her next words.

"Don't be silly," she said with a smirk. "Who's ever heard of a praying mantis eating *before* sex?" She inched closer, her faceted, emerald eyes gazing softly at his smooth skin. He closed his eyes as her mouth brushed against his ear. Her hot breath tickled him, made his heart race. A long tongue slithered out of her lipless mouth to lick his slender neck. "That would *ruin* my appetite."

Infinite Waters

"Not fair!" she shouted and leaned back on her chair, giggling. "That was too short!"

"You said you wanted one last story."

"I still do! That was no story, that was just a teaser."

I rubbed the back of my neck. "Fine. But be careful what you wish for."

Infinite Waters: 9+1 Speculative Fiction Short Stories

Would You Like Flies With That?

I let out a small groan at the number of people queuing in front of the butcher's stall. Once again, everyone had waited until the last moment to do their Halloween shopping, and the super market was surprisingly crowded. I shuffled into the queue. A small, bald man with a funny polka dot bowtie was staring absent-mindedly at a pig's head behind the glass. Someone had placed a Halloween piece next to it; a spooky jack-o'-lantern that flashed its toothless grin at me. The thing gave me the creeps and I took out my frustration on the little man, shoving him aside. If he wasn't planning on ordering anything, he shouldn't be standing there, right?

The man squeaked a protest, but a glare and a bulge of my biceps made him shut his mouth. He tapped my elbow as if to say everything was alright and shuffled away.

I scoffed and ignored him, my mind fixed on more serious matters: my girlfriend. Well, that's not true: Lea had me parked in the friend zone for so long, I'd become a permanent fixture there, like an abandoned, derelict car gathering crumbling leaves and dust at the corner of a back street. I, on the other hand, spent every waking minute—and many a sleeping one—aching for her, longing for her to see me as anything but her BFF.

I sighed as my gaze drifted back to the pig's head. Its eyes seemed to follow me, and I shifted my weight uncomfortably between my feet, trying to avoid its dead stare. Then, it blinked.

Sweat erupted on my forehead and I shuddered, my stomach suddenly lurching. I gaped at the head, and it met my stare with surprisingly lively eyes. Then it blinked again and a faint smile played on its thin lips. I jolted back, bumping into a butcher carrying a whole lamb from the freezer.

"Oy, watch it, mate!" he said, then noticed my pallor. "You okay?"

I opened my mouth to speak, then my eyes met those of the lamb on his back. It nodded at me in greeting. A scream caught in my throat. *I must be hallucinating*, I thought. *Yes, that must be it.* I steadied myself and drew deep breaths, struggling to ignore the lively carcasses around me. The lamb whistled a tune and the man shot me a curious glance before disappearing into the back. Pushing back in line, I stared dead ahead, hiding my shivering hands in my pockets.

The woman in front of me pushed her glasses up the bridge of her nose and leaned forward, only a thin sliver of glass between her nose and the pig's snout. She tapped the glass, a smile crawling on her face. A bead of sweat trickled down my temples as it lifted its eyes to stare at her. She cooed in appreciation and wiggled playful fingers, as if to attract its attention.

This was all too much for me. My trolley forgotten by the butcher's, I backpedalled to the exit, my eyes never leaving the chuckling woman. When the automatic door opened, I spun around to welcome the brisk autumn air on my face. Still shaking, I stumbled towards the parking assistant on my way to my car, when I noticed a van parked by the back entrance. I stole an absent-minded look inside and froze in my tracks at the sight of a dozen calves hanging from shiny hooks, skinned and bloodless. One of them turned its head and gave me an awkward smile, as if to apologize for its state. I swear, had its feet been untied, it would have covered up itself in modesty.

Raising my fist to my mouth to stifle a shriek, I stumbled towards my car, my other hand rummaging in my pocket for the keys.

"Excuse me," the butcher I had nearly bumped into yelled at me, as he exited the store. Why was he following me? I lowered my head and hastened my step. "Excuse me," he repeated, catching the parking assistant's attention. Out of the corner of my downcast eyes I caught the new threat's shiny yellow vest as he moved to intercept me, standing between me and my car.

I bolted to the left, almost crashing into a sports car exiting the parking lot. "Watch it!" the man inside yelled as he slammed on the brakes. The car screeched to a halt.

I yanked his door open and grabbed him. Thankfully, he was not wearing a seatbelt and in my terror I had little trouble hauling him out of the car. "What are you doing?" the female passenger screamed as I jumped into his seat.

"Get out," I said, then noticed a bag filled with meat in her hands. *She must be one of them!*

"You get out!" she screamed and lunged at me. She let out a pained cry as her seatbelt jolted her back. I ignored her, my eyes glued in the mirror at the sight of the butcher rushing at the car. If he caught me, they'd drag me back to the shop, back to the... things. Without a second thought, I hit the gas. The car vaulted forward with the power of a couple hundred horses, slamming us into our seats. "What are you doing?" she cried out.

I had no time to deal with her as I swerved to avoid the parking assistant, wheels shrieking in anger. He flew into a fake witch hovering on her broomstick and I shot before him, the car's engine roaring. The smell of burnt rubber filled my nostrils, but I dared not slow down as we hit the ramp to the road. Sparks flew out of the low car upon its impact with the asphalt, the engine protesting with a deafening howl. "Let me out!" the woman next to me yelled.

"Too late now," I said through gritted teeth. My mind raced. How many people knew of this? And when did it happen? When did everyone start eating live meat? How could the animals be alive, when skinned and exsanguinated? I shot a sideways glance at the woman, wondering if she had any answers, and nodded towards the bag she was clutching in her hands. "What's inside?"

"Meat?" she stammered.

"What kind?"

She stole a glance at the bag. "Chicken." I sighed with relief. I had not noticed any live poultry. "And pork."

I almost crashed the car on a telephone pole, swerving at the last moment. Bile rose to my throat. "So you know," I growled.

"Know what?" she protested, her face draining of colour. It reminded me too much of the animals in the van, and I shut my eyes to chase the image away. "Watch out!" she screamed, and my eyes flew open again. I slammed the brakes to avoid crashing into the back of a truck. The car came to a screeching halt, my heart thudding in my chest.

"Get out," I growled. This time she obeyed me without a word. I floored the gas as soon as both her feet were on the road, and inertia slammed the door shut. The last I saw of her as the car roared away, she was staring at me bug-eyed. *I'm not the crazy one! You're the one eating live meat!*

I took the ramp to the motorway. I had to get away, gather my thoughts. Who else knew? Then, my pocket vibrated and a second later my phone rang. I had completely forgotten about it. *I could ask for help. But who would help me?* I fished it out of my pocket to glance at the screen.

I swallowed hard and tried to clear my head before swiping my thumb over the screen. "Hi, Lea."

"Hey!" My breath caught at the sound of her voice. "Where are you?"

"Long story." I slowed down and swerved behind a truck. The last thing I needed was to get pulled over for speeding.

"Listen..." She paused. "We need to talk."

I cringed. No good had ever come from those words. I tried to keep my voice neutral, casual. "What about?"

"Well..." She hesitated. "How you feel about me." *Shit. Not cool.* "And how I feel about you."

My heart skipped a beat. "How do you mean?"

"I know we've been friends for so long, but what if I wanted more?"

Was it me, or was it getting warm in the car? "Are you..." I cleared the lump from my throat. "Are you saying you want more?"

"Why don't you come over and we can discuss it?" she said in her bedroom voice.

I almost did a 180 right then and there, forgetting I was on the motorway, then it hit me. All these months I've been waiting for this, and it happened now? Just as I had stumbled on something this big?

"Sounds good," I said cautiously. "I'll see you at your place in ten."

"Ah..." She sounded apprehensive. "How about the burger joint, instead? You know, the new one? They say the burgers there are to die for."

A chill touched the base of my spine and travelled all the way up to my scalp. I opened the window and threw the phone out. I had watched enough movies to know that's how they find you. *Not Lea, too!* My eyes moistened, and I wiped them with one hand, squeezing the steering wheel with the other until my knuckles turned white. Crap, if they've gotten to her, that means they're everywhere!

I took deep breaths and ran my sweaty palm through my hair as I passed a police car, a copper holding a radar gun. I knew I was driving below the limit, but he looked up to stare at me. *He knows! Maybe he's one of them!* Trying my best to keep the car at an even speed, I waited until he had disappeared, then continued driving as far from that place as possible.

The sun had set by the time I swerved off the motorway into an exit, then into a back road. A classmate of mine lived nearby. I had not seen him in years, but he was a vegetarian. I should be safe there. Reaching a junction, I took a left, then came back as I reached a dead end. This time I turned right, to arrive at a nice farmhouse with a large garden, filled with growing, leafy vegetables. Golden fruit filled the trees of an orchard at the back.

I parked before his gate and stared at my fingers clutching the steering wheel, my mind spinning faster than the still-running engine. After an eternity, I turned it off and stepped out of the car, leaving the stolen keys in the ignition.

I stepped out of the car on unsteady legs and drank the crisp evening air with hungry breaths. A handful of early stars shimmered in the sky, providing some much-needed illumination. *I wish he'd turn on a light!* I covered the short distance to the porch with slow steps. My feet kicked up small drifts, ribboned by the wind. I needed to sober up, my head stuffed with wool and crowded with too many thoughts. As my finger touched the buzzer, an impatient hand tapped my shoulder.

I let out a startled yelp and spun around to see an irate older woman holding a red, plastic basket. "Are you ordering anything?" Her nasal voice grated my frayed nerves.

I blinked repeatedly to shake away my confusion before raising my eyes to look at the long queue behind her. I was back at the butcher's stall, a dozen people glaring at me, mumbling under their breath. "Come on, we ain't got all day," someone muttered, and people murmured in agreement.

"I'm..." I swallowed the lump in my throat. "I'm sorry." I turned to face the butcher. "I'd like..." My gaze fell on the pig's head, the one that had triggered the unsettling waking nightmare. "Erm, you haven't got any vegetarian sausages now, do you?"

Behind me, two girls giggled. A wave of anger hit me at the thought they were mocking me, but when I spun around to face them, they were staring at the small man with the polka dot bowtie. Had he been standing next to me all this time?

"I'm telling you, that's him," one of the girls said in an excited, hushed whisper. "Doctor Hypnosis himself—the world's greatest illusionist!"

"And crusader against rudeness," he muttered as he passed me by to approach the girls, a wide smile spreading across his face.

I opened my mouth to speak, but my gaze caught on the pig's head. I took a double take and my heart almost stopped. I could swear that the jack-o'-lantern had winked at the pig in approval.

Infinite Waters

She gaped at me. I could see goosebumps on her arms. "That was... disturbing." Her fingers grazed mine. "Perhaps one more? Something funny?"

I shook my head from side to side. "No." With careful fingers, I placed the crystal ball inside its fabric prison and under the table once again.

"But—"

I raised one finger to stop her. "I can, however, tell you whether you'll find success or not."

She hesitated for a moment, then nodded furiously, smothering the leather bag against her chest. "Yes," she squeaked. "Please."

With half-closed eyes, I let my hand hover over my other tools. I allowed an imperceptible pull to guide my fingers, until they rubbed against the cards. Lifting them gently, I shuffled the deck. Sympathy tugged at my heart. I hoped the cards would tell her what she wanted to hear. This book of hers might be her last chance at success; her last chance of happiness.

I held the cards on my palm and extended my arm. She shot me a questioning look. "Draw," I said. She did so reluctantly, as if her very future depended on it. First a single, apprehensive card, followed by several more, each more confident than the previous one. She placed them all on the small round table, spreading them out like a fan.

"Thank you," I said, and emptied my mind as my fingertips grazed the first card. When I upturned it, an impish smile made my mouth twitch. It widened into a grin with the next ones. Only the last card troubled me, and I closed my eyes while working out the best way to share with her the future whispered to me by the archetypal images.

"You will be very successful," I started. She fought a squeal of pleasure and jolted so hard that the plastic pin in her hair gave up in desperation, allowing half of her sweet-smelling hair to burst around her neck. I could not help but smile; she looked ten—no—twenty years younger already. She looked downright beautiful, and I felt another tug on my heart.

"In fact, your book will be taught at schools and universities," I continued, enjoying how her baby blue eyes widened with each word. "It will be read by book clubs everywhere. You, my dear, are a very talented author." I stressed the last three words, staring into her startled eyes.

She let out a deep breath and collapsed listless on her chair. For a moment I feared the shock had proven too much for her, but then she jumped to her feet and lunged at me. Before I had a chance to stop her, she had her arms around me, squeezing me like a teddy bear.

"Oh, thank you, thank you, thank you," she said, planting wet kisses on my cheek. "You don't know how much this means to me! Nobody believes in me, even my sister thinks I'm just..." Her voice trailed off. I fought an unexpected sense of loss when she released me to pat down my clothes in embarrassment. "Thank you," she repeated, flashing me a huge grin before pushing the awning aside to bolt outside, a newfound spring in her step.

The wind flapped the tent, almost drowning out the sounds from the crowded fair that seeped in. I brought the awning back down, fastening it absent-mindedly with a cord.

I debated hurrying after her to share the rest of the future revealed to me, then decided against it. I would meet her again soon enough, and if she knew that success would take almost a century to find her, she might never finish her work.

A smile flickered on my lips. At least she had now met the tall, dark stranger promised by the cards, and I would do everything in my power to keep that gorgeous smile on her face for the rest of her days. If the cards were right—and they had never lied to me—she would not mind life in the carnival in the least.

Further Stories

If you enjoyed these short stories, you may also enjoy *The Power of Six: 6+1 Science Fiction Short Stories*. You can read a short story from that collection below.

Infinite Waters: 9+1 Speculative Fiction Short Stories

The Power of Six: 6+1 Science Fiction Short Stories

Infinite Waters: 9+1 Speculative Fiction Short Stories

The Hand of God

The bartender rubbed a soiled glass with a dirty towel, not quite sure which one was cleaning the other. The bar might be a dusty, crummy drinking hole, but it was the closest one to the Academy. As such, it was busy every evening, as soon as the cadets were allowed to leave the walled premises. He stole a glance at his watch; soon the bar would fill with uniforms.

A chuckle made him look up at the only full table. A bunch of cadets had gathered around the Veteran to listen to his story. The bartender had to admit the old man knew how to hold a crowd's interest. He'd better; he must have told that story a million times in exchange for a drink.

The Veteran had just started his tale. Staring into his empty glass, his eyes opened as if he was watching the Beasts approach once more.

"You see, girls, things were different back then. Nowadays, each colony has its Academy and barracks in every major city. Back then, mankind had built a vast fleet of transports, but only a handful of military ships, safe in the illusion of its uniqueness."

A cute redhead with freckles interrupted him. "Surely you suspected we were not alone." She scrunched her face as a blonde with short hair dug her elbow into the redhead's ribs to stop her.

The Veteran continued as if he had not been interrupted. "We were finally at peace after millennia of conflict. No one was prepared for the shock of encountering a hostile alien species; so alien, that communication was impossible. When we lost contact with the more remote colonies, we thought it was a glitch with our transmitters. As one colony after another fell silent, we sent ships. Not military ones, either. We had too few of those." He took a napkin to his forehead to wipe beads of sweat and looked suggestively at the empty glass.

"Can we have one more over here?" the blonde yelled across the bar, without even bothering to look at the bartender.

A sweet smile played on the Veteran's lips, and he licked them in anticipation. "Thank you, my love. Now, as I was saying, when the ships disappeared as well, we realized we had become complacent. I still remember the day we first saw the Beasts. A boy had beaten the odds to send us a video of their attack. I was a designer back then, waiting to go into a meeting. One of the secretaries rushed into the meeting room to switch the vid on. The poor thing aged ten years in a single moment."

The girls around him leaned away to allow the barman to deliver the man's drink. The Veteran picked it up with slightly trembling fingers and swirled the amber liquid around, careful not to spill a drop. He listened to the clink of the ice cubes, the tips of his lips curling upwards.

"Meanwhile, even more colonies fell silent," he continued. "We dropped everything to prepare for the invasion. Colonies were evacuated, millions of people returning to the welcoming cradle of mother Earth. Only, it wasn't a haven, but a tomb. Or at least that's what we thought back then, as one line of defence crumbled after another. I fought in almost all of the big battles, losing every single one of them. 'We haven't lost yet', we'd tell each other. 'We'll get 'em next time.' Until they entered the Solar System, crushing the Jupiter garrison, then the Mars one, then finally reached the moon. Not the sorry affair you see in the sky nowadays; it was a full, nice round moon back then."

He took a swish of the drink and swirled it in his mouth, before plonking the glass back onto the table. Smacking his lips for a moment, he lost himself in memories of a full moon. "The moon was our last line of defence. After that, there was nothing but women and children on Earth. It was down to us to stop them."

The Veteran drew a line on the dirty table, pushing the fine dust with his finger to mark small dots. "They had kicked us out of each planet we had colonized, but this was different," he snarled. "This time, we were fighting for our home. If we failed, nothing could save humanity. Next stop, Earth."

He glanced at the wide eyes of his audience, hanging on his every word. "If you think that's what was on my mind as we landed, you're wrong. All I cared about was making it out of there alive. I don't care what those teachers of yours tell you at the Academy; not even half of us made it to the moon. The rest, deserters. Some wanted to stay back on Earth to die with their families. Others took off for any corner of the universe with a rock they could crawl under, thinking they'd wait it all out."

He cast a triumphant look around him, as if he dared them to contradict his story. In fact, less than 20% had deserted, but his claim made him feel special; brave.

Turning his attention back to the dusty line on the table, he continued. "We were deployed along the Line. The engineers had already dropped the bunkers while in orbit, so we moved in as fast as we could, followed by Blacks and Tourists."

He shot a questioning glance at his audience, but they seemed familiar with the slang for the armoured units and air support. They probably knew that infantry was referred to as Dirts, too, but no one pointed it out to him. Besides, the animosity between the various units held fast even today. Back then it was worse; everyone really hated armoured units. Their missiles were notoriously unreliable, half of them missing their target to land among the infantry. In many battles, the Beasts only had to finish off the remains of infantry units blown to bits by friendly fire.

"There was so much dust around us, we could not see anything without infrared goggles. Central Command had sent everyone old enough to hold a rifle to stand on the Line. They knew we wouldn't get a second chance; one mistake, and humanity's gone. I was fighting alongside kids younger than you. Most had never seen a Beast up close, let alone survive one's attack. I was the senior in my bunker, and the only real veteran. The oldest one after that had seen no action in two years."

He took another gulp and wiped his unshaven chin with his napkin. A look of pride crossed his face for a moment, followed by a dark cloud.

"There is no sound in space, you know. Sounds need air to travel, but there's no air on the moon. There is air in spacesuits, though. And microphones." He flinched, a brief spasm crossing his wrinkled face. "When the Beasts attack, you hear your friends scream and the rip in their suits as they get torn apart, but the Beast slaughtering them moves in the vacuum of space, making no sound."

"But we've heard the Beasts on the vids," the freckled redhead blurted out with an involuntary shudder. "They sound like thunder."

"The vids…" He pushed trembling fingers through the thinning hair on his head. "Sound can only travel through objects. When a beast impales a man, the microphones pick up its roar as a deep rumble. Beasts don't breathe; it's pulsing membranes in their neck that make the sound. That's what you've heard." He turned his bloodshot eyes at her, their gaze locking until she turned her head away. "In the absence of physical contact, however, it makes no difference whether a Beast is standing a hundred yards or an inch away; you still can't hear it. The lack of atmosphere serves as sound insulation. So, we only knew they were coming when the motion-activated spotlights lit up the darkness around us. When the lights behind us lit up, too, we froze. No one understood how they could be attacking from both sides. We later found out they could burrow underground, but it was the first time they had used that strategy. Either that, or the Generals back on Earth couldn't tell back from forth."

Once again, he enjoyed the cadets' shocked expressions. Coming from someone else, a jibe against the most decorated soldiers in history would be considered treason. Their new President was but a Colonel back then; she was one of the few people to have survived the Line. The Veteran was one of only a handful of people who could speak his mind about her, and he loved his freedom.

He dug his fist into a bowl filled with nuts and brought them to his mouth. After washing the salty flavour with a sip of his drink, he continued.

"Once the shock passed, we threw everything we had at them. Bullets, missiles, grenades, our knickers, anything we could lay our hands on. Our bunker was lit up like a Christmas tree by the explosions and the flares, lighting up their ugly faces. Two Blacks flanking us disappeared under a wave of Beasts, leaving behind only charred remains. A Tourist almost crashed into our bunker, downed by acid-spitting Beasts. Outside, hell itself had broken loose. All I could see were explosions and the thin lines left by tracer bullets. We felt more than heard a dull thud, and I spun around to see our door cave in under their blows. As I turned my rifle against the Beasts storming in, I remember thinking, 'This is it; it can't get no worse than this.' When I saw a Queen standing so close to me I could touch her, I knew I was wrong."

He paused for another sip, raising the glass to his lips with shaking hands, terror filling his eyes. The cadets exchanged looks of doubt, but he did not mind. He knew what they were thinking. *Could he really have seen a Beast Queen and lived to tell the tale?* This was not the part that scared him to death, though; the part that woke him up screaming in the middle of the night. That part was coming.

"So? What happened next?" the freckled redhead asked after a while, her voice betraying her impatience.

Her voice returned him to reality, and he turned his gaze at her. She took an involuntary step back, hit by the strength of his glare. "What no one wants to admit," he growled. "I saw the hand of God himself, is what happened!"

The cadet stared back at him, her look betraying her bemusement, but she dared not open her mouth.

"I don't care if you believe me, I know what I saw," he yelled and slammed the glass down, sending a cloud of dust to twirl inside a thin ray of afternoon light dancing on the table. He studied his hand until it stopped shaking. After a moment he continued, his voice a low growl again. "I know what I saw. Letters sliced the night like a knife. They were huge—bigger than a juggernaut! One after another, filling out the sky; only the wrong way around, like seen through a mirror. But crystal clear. Everything froze; I could not move, as if time itself had stopped by the strange words, written by the hand of God himself."

He did not pause to see if anyone believed him. No one did, save for those on the Line; and most of them had tried to forget. Not him, though. He knew what he had seen, and had to tell everyone. "Time started its relentless flow again," he continued, "only this time a white light engulfed me. I stared at my hands, trying to figure it out, too shocked to notice the Queen lunging at me. Not just me, all humans were glowing in that same light. Out of the corner of my eye I caught a huge tail whipping towards me, and I winced, expecting it to slice my body in half. Instead, it passed right through me." He tapped a finger at the table, repeating every word. "Right through me!"

He shook his head and stared at the young girls, daring them to doubt him. No one spoke. "I don't know who was more surprised; her or me. I'd run out of rifle ammo, so I fumbled with my sidearm and shot at her. I swear, I expected the bullet to barely scratch her. This is a Queen we're talking about; I'd seen them survive missile attacks. And yet, as soon as my bullet hit her, she exploded! A boy in the bunker got caught up in the moment; so much so that he threw a grenade, not realizing we'd be caught in the blast. I yelled to stop him, but I was too late. The explosion nearly deafened me, but when the smoke cleared, we were all alive, standing over bloodied Beast bits.

We could not understand what was going on, and crawled out of the bunker. Outside, the few surviving men and women were bathed in the white light, and for the first time we killed Beasts faster than their Queens could spew them. We soon started our counterattack, claiming back first the moon, then clearing out the rest of the galaxy. It was the moment when everything changed, yet no one dares speak of it." He banged an angry fist on the table, raising more dust.

The blonde cleared her throat. "We were shown vids from the Line at the Academy. It was the President's strategy that—"

He cut her off with a tired wave of his hand. "Yeah, yeah, that must have been it. She saved the day. Bah!"

The cadets exchanged awkward looks. "What are you still doing here?" he asked them. "That's the story. There's nothing more to say. Now scram. Leave me alone."

The redhead patted him on the back as the girls moved back to their table, leaving the old man to his thoughts. The blonde made a circling motion with a finger against her temple and winked at the redhead, who nodded and chuckled, stealing a look at the Veteran, hoping he had not caught that. She need not have worried; he had bigger problems than a bunch of doubting cadets. He had seen the hand of God. He knew the world for what it really was.

The bartender standing next to him caught his attention. The young man pointed at the L-shaped medal hanging around the Veteran's neck. "On the house," he said and plonked a half-full bottle on the table, throwing a look of pity at the old man. The old man grunted his thanks as he poured the liquid into his glass. He stared at it, shaking his head and muttering to himself.

###

Mark glanced at the blinking cursor on his monitor, a wicked smile playing on his lips as he punched his keyboard. He paused for a second to check the message his mate had sent him; the one with the cheat code. "Cheat: godMode enable;" appeared on the screen. He hit enter, and the cursor blinked, along with a new message: "Cheat active. God mode enabled."

"Let's see how you like this, you suckers," he mumbled under his breath and unpaused the game.

A Note from the Author

These short stories were written between 2014 and 2015, as a break from working on my epic fantasy series, *Pearseus*, and my children's books, *Runaway Smile* and *Musiville*. Much like the stories in my previous collection of short stories, *The Power of Six*, they aim to poke holes at the fabric of reality, hopefully eliciting a chuckle or two in the process.

Everyone has their own theory about Greek gods, from aliens to Atlantis refugees. "The Things We Do for Lust" offers a light-hearted alternative. Trekkies will probably enjoy the many Star Trek references.

"James' Life" is lighter in nature, despite the heaviness. What if video technology evolved to the point of the characters having their own feelings about what was happening to them? How happy would they be repeating the same mistakes night after night?

The idea behind "Two's a Crowd" came to me from a comic I read as a young teenager. A man has a recurring nightmare. Every single night he fights axe-wielding monsters in a bloodied battlefield. When a monster kills him and the police find his body, they are baffled as to why anyone would commit murder with a large axe. However, once again, it is the nature of reality that's really questioned here. "Am I a butterfly dreaming I am a man, or a man dreaming I am a butterfly?", as Chuang Chou put it.

I thought of "What's in a Name?" while listening to *Little Blue* by *The Beautiful South*. Paul Heaton and Jacqui Abbott have the most wonderful lyrics, and this lovely line really stuck to my head: "You don't name your boat Titanic II." That's when it hit me: what if you did?

I was going through a rough patch when I thought of "The Lucky Bastard." Life can throw us a whole lot of curveballs, but where would we be without them? Would someone who has led a perfect life be happy, or deeply miserable, unable to enjoy and appreciate any of their achievements?

"A Twist of the Tail" came to me while reading on Alzheimer's. What if the warped reality of those suffering from this terrible disease is actually based on fact? What if we pity them only because we can't see the full picture?

"Is There a Doctor in the House?" is the tongue-in-cheek story of Doctor Frankenstein's son. What would he be like, as an awkward teenager? Would he continue his father's experiments?

"Sex and Dinner" was a Valentine's special I wrote for my blog, based on an idea by my friends, Thomas Doxiadis and Sam Levis. We were laughing at all the strange ways nature has found to procreate. Naturally, this led to the question of why the male mantis prefers to risk getting eaten to staying single.

"Would You Like Files With That" is pretty much copied verbatim from a strange dream I had. I simply added the Halloween aspects when I published it on my blog as a Halloween special.

Finally, I wrote "It's in the Cards" as a contribution to the _Rave Soup for the Writer's Soul_ anthology. It was published there in December 2014, and became the container for these other stories under the new title, "Infinite Waters".

Readers of my stories will have noticed my disdain for names, both for characters and places, whenever possible. This is because of my conviction that names inevitably restrict the reader's imagination. We all carry deep in our psyche an image for all names and places and this will necessarily carry on to the story, limiting the possible projections we can perform. I'd rather leave the canvas completely blank so that readers can colour it any way they like.

Infinite Waters: 9+1 Speculative Fiction Short Stories

About the Author

Nicholas Rossis lives to write and does so from his cottage on the edge of a magical forest in Athens, Greece. When not composing epic fantasies or short sci-fi stories, he chats with fans and colleagues, writes blog posts, walks his dog, and enjoys the antics of two silly cats, one of whom claims his lap as home.  His children's book, Runaway Smile, earned a finalist slot in the 2015 International Book Awards.

Nicholas is all around the Internet, but the best place to connect with him would be on his blog, http://nicholasrossis.me/

Anyone interested in his books can check them out on Amazon:

http://www.amazon.com/Nicholas-C.-Rossis/e/B00FXXIBZA/

People can read *Runaway Smile* for free on http://nicholasrossis.me/childrens-books/

Infinite Waters: 9+1 Speculative Fiction Short Stories

Acknowledgments

They say that everyone has a book in them. What they don't say is how much it helps if you're not alone in your attempts to share your words with the world.

Many thanks to my excellent editor, Lorelei Logsdon; my friend and beta-reader MMJaye and all my wonderful ARC reviewers and friends.

A special thanks to all the new friends I've made on social media, and to my readers—this endeavor would be meaningless without you. And a very special thanks to my fiercest critic and greatest help, my wife Electra.

Infinite Waters: 9+1 Speculative Fiction Short Stories

Further Notes

If you enjoyed *Infinite Rivers*, you may be interested in *The Power of Six: 6+1 Science Fiction Short Stories*, available on Amazon:

http://amzn.to/1E00JED

Want to contact me? Eager for an e-book autograph?

Follow me on http://nicholasrossis.me

For every new follower,

my dog does a happy dance… :)

If you wish to report a typo or have reviewed this book on Amazon, please email *info@nicholasrossis.com* with the word "review" on the subject line, to receive a free 1680x1050 Pearseus desktop background.

Infinite Waters: 9+1 Speculative Fiction Short Stories

Thank you for taking the time to read *Infinite Waters*! If you enjoyed it, please consider telling your friends or posting a short review. Word of mouth is an author's best friend and much appreciated.

This is an original work of fiction. Any relationship to real people is unintentional and a coincidence.

Printed in Great Britain
by Amazon